More Than Mushrooms

AMY LAURENS

OTHER WORKS

Find other works by the author at www.amylaurens.com

More Than Mushrooms

INKLET #91

AMY LAURENS

www.inkprintpress.com

Print ISBN: 978-1-922434-31-9
eBook ISBN: 9798201020408

www.inkprintpress.com

National Library of Australia Cataloguing-in-Publication Data
Laurens, Amy 1985 –
More Than Mushrooms
54 p.
ISBN: 978-1-922434-31-9
Inkprint Press, Canberra, Australia
1. Fiction—Family Life—General 2. Fiction—Short Stories

First Print Edition: October 2022
Cover photo © DanaTentis via Pixabay
Cover design © Inkprint Press
Interior art © Amy Laurens

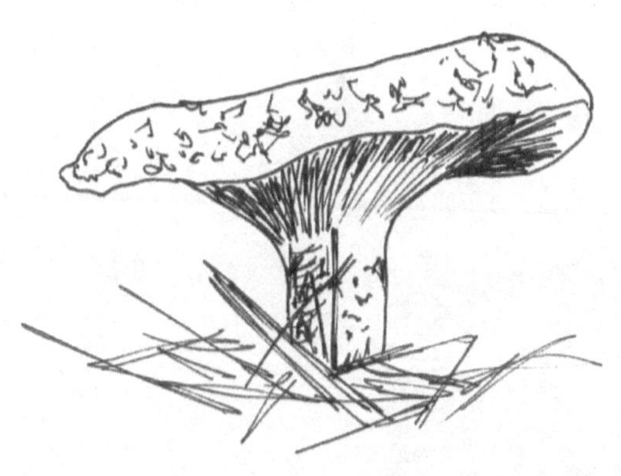

MORE THAN
MUSHROOMS

THE SILENCE WAS NOT GOLDEN, BE-cause the breeze was just a little too fresh for that, but it was definitely silver, or some other kind of precious stone. It was the kind of silence you only got out of doors, away from the buzz and hum of city electricity, away from *humanity*.

Lily, as an extrovert and an optimist, generally approved of humanity. But she defied even the most optimistic extrovert to remain entirely upbeat after three straight weeks house-bound with two small kids and a restless husband, whose introverted nature was taking a pounding.

Hence: the silver silence of the outdoors.

Here, in this secluded gully full of knee-high bracken fern, bordered by radiata pines in drunken, staggering rows, the wind was the only thing Lily could hear right now, and as cliched as it felt to call it that, it was utterly refreshing.

Somewhere down below, at the bottom of the gentle slope a hundred or so metres away, were her husband and the kids. They hadn't gone far, just beyond sight, with but the pine branches hiding them and the wind sweeping their chatter away from her, Lily might just as well be alone.

She smiled. Leaned back on her wrists, adjusting one as it slipped a little on the emerald sleeping bag they had brought from the car as a make-shift picnic rug, the actual picnic rug that lived there having gone temporarily and mysteriously missing.

In front of her, a little cloud of midges investigated the mostly empty plastic picnic cups, the last dregs of pink milk in the bottom of them apparently intriguing the little insects. The taste of the milk still hung at the edges of her mouth, sweet and sugary like decadence and family intimacy.

The breeze changed directions for a moment, and Lily wrinkled her nose at a familiar smell: she'd spent quite a bit of time hiking around in pine plantations, and every so often this smell, the one that smelled like the kids had left the toilet unflushed after a particularly intense episode of use, reared its head.

It wasn't quite like poo, she allowed, turning it over in her mind as she inhaled. How would she describe it? Poo-ish. A little more like dirt. Like decay. Perhaps a touch mildewy or mushroomy.

The mushroom bit might make sense. Half the reason they were here, after all, was that her husband had gotten it into his head that he wanted to try mushroom hunting, come after the saffron milk caps that had an apparent affinity with pine forests the world over. They were easily identified, moderately easy to find, and reportedly quite tasty, according to a bunch of local YouTubers.

Benjamin, their eight-year-old, had supported the idea with unbridled enthusiasm. And both the kids needed a run, and Lily was happy to get out in the fresh air, and so after double-checking the permissibility of their actions, here they were.

Thank goodness the national parks were still open in their area.

Lily breathed deeply again, feeling the tension drain away from her shoulders, her chest.

There hadn't been any mushrooms here at the top of the gully, and maybe her family would have more luck down in the bottom where they'd gone exploring, but even if they returned home empty handed, not a one of them would return home empty-souled.

And at this point, that was all Lily could ask of the world: all she wanted was for the kids to get through this with a minimum of trauma, for them to be happy.

Another deep breath—the air fresh and clean again now, the wind having swung back around—and Lily smiled. A tiny slice of heaven, that's what this was.

Her gaze lit on something across the other side of the gentle gully, maybe ten, fifteen metres away just in the border of the pines. The rusty needles were lifted and scuffed in places, as though perhaps a new crop of mushrooms were rearing their heads underneath—they'd check, but the only ones they'd found in that area so far were slippery jacks, with their spongey yellow undersides, and her husband was a little suspicious of eating those even though they were, notionally, edible—and just there, a couple of trees back in a hollow between the dry, needleless lower branches, was something vibrantly green.

Lily stared, curious but too languorous to get up and investigate. Too bright for anything natural, it was a limey-sort of green, and shiny. Probably litter, from prior mushroom hunters. Her husband had said after his preliminary investigation that it did look like others had been here recently.

Litter made sense.

A shout from the bottom of the gully drew Lily's attention; it was Benjamin, reappearing in his black shirt and camo pants that he'd picked out especially for their 'adventure'. She had no idea what had piqued his attention—not that it took much for him to raise his voice, they were constantly reminding him that 'inside voices' were a Thing—but his body language was animated and joyful, and it brought a smile to Lily's face.

His dark hair was getting long; they'd have to break out the clippers tonight.

His sister appeared through the pines behind him, entirely inappropriately dressed in unicorn jeans and a too-thin shirt for the weather, her hand tightly clasped in her father's. She was chatting animatedly too as Russell swung her up and over a blackberry bramble, nearly bare-caned as winter approached.

With a sigh that weighed more of contentment than resignation, Lily scrambled to her feet and began re-packing their makeshift picnic away in the orange reusable shopping bag that had served as a basket.

She rolled the chip packets down with a crinkle, tucked them into the bag and licked her fingers, stealing the last skerrick of salty, vinegary flavour.

The last cheese roll, the rest of the pink milk, the half box of end-of-season plums that had been on sale in the corner store…

Lily gathered it all back into the bag and straightened, hands on her lower back as she leaned side to side and stretched.

That lime green thing in the fringe of the pines still bothered her. There really was no excuse for littering ex-cept laziness, and she'd been trained early and often about the magnitude of that particular sin. One didn't live in debt to others if one could at all avoid it.

With a little sniff outward through her nose, Lily left the shopping bag with the sleeping bag-turned-picnic mat and picked her way through the sporadic brambles and bracken fern across the head of the gully.

She smiled wryly as she passed a slippery jack her son had kicked over, exposing its spongy yellow underside to the sun. It didn't especially bother her if they found no edible mushrooms today. On the one hand, she was pretty confident that the saffron milk caps were hard to misidentify.

On the other... Well, it was eating wild mushrooms.

Under the fringes of the trees, where a frond of needles prickled at her forehead and the wind felt cool, the lime green thing sparkled on the ground, nestled by a stray tussock of vibrant grass and half covered by a little hump of rust-coloured needles. Lily bent, frowning. She'd thought at first it might have been a chip packet or some such, that shiny, metallic-looking material that was actually just disguised plastic.

But no. It *looked* like a chip packet or some such, but it was completely blank, no branding, no labels, nothing. And it looked thicker than the metallic plastic stuff they used for chips, a synthetic leather or something per-haps.

She picked it up, surprised at the weight of the little pouch, about twice the size of one of those little individual serves of chips. Definitely some sort of fake leather-like fabric, with some-thing sort of knobbly inside. But darn if she could open the thing—there didn't seem to be any trace of a zipper or press studs or anything as she turned it over in her hands. Only a neat and definite row of thick stitching across one end—professional, though, like it had been made that way, not like someone had done it at home with a needle or machine.

Behind her, halfway down the gully, the children shrieked with laughter.

Lily whipped around toward them, blinking. For a second, she'd forgotten she wasn't alone.

Frown weighing down her lips, knotting her eyebrows, she paced back out of the trees again and waited while Russell hiked the last of the way through the brambles and ferns with little Angel swinging in his arms.

It had grown darker, and Lily glanced up at the inclement clouds. A good moment to make their exit.

Sure enough, as Russell approached, fitful rain began to spit from the sky, teeny tiny droplets bearing an icy prickle that belied their size.

"What have you got there?" Russell asked as he drew near. He popped

Angel down on the ground—she giggled—"Again, Daddy! Again!"—and came to Lily.

He smelled of clean sweat and pine, and instinctively Lily took half a step closer so they stood shoulder-to-shoulder. "I don't know," Lily said. "A pouch or something. I found it just over there in the trees. It doesn't seem to open."

Wordlessly, Russell accepted it from her and turned it over and over, squeezing it gently and holding it up to his ear to hear the gentle clinkish sort of sound. He shrugged, handed it back. "No clue," he said. "Someone must have left it here."

Lily rolled her eyes. "Well *obviously*, I highly doubt it grew here."

Russell grinned.

"What do I do with it?"

Russell shrugged again. "No clue," he said, and turned away to snag Benjamin as he went pelting past. "Hey, kiddo, grab the sleeping bag will you, it's time to go."

"Awwww." Benjamin pouted, but picked up the sleeping bag regardless, bunching it up in his arms with a rustling sound almost like feathers.

Rain splattered it erratically, little dark spots on the deep green of the synthetic fabric.

"I'll take it with us," Lily said, tucking the strange green pouch into their orange shopping bag anyway. "Even if it's rubbish, it should go in a bin."

Russell smiled fondly at her over Angel's dark hair; he'd picked Angel up again and was holding her parallel with the ground over his shoulder as she shrieked with delight. "Sure," he said. "Whatever makes you happy."

Lily shook her head, half exasperated as ever at her husband's lackadaisical approach to litter, and half in love, as ever, with his willingness to do whatever did make her happy.

They bundled their way up the remainder of the slope to where they'd left the car on the side of the orange-dirt road, packed in their things and then the children, and head back for town.

At home that night, after the children were in bed and Lily and Russell were tucked up on the leather couch under a couple of blankets watching TV, Lily tipped her head back against the lounge and closed her eyes. "I think I'll put a message up on Facebook or something," she said.

She wriggled her toes under the blankets, pleased at how quickly they had warmed up; the air tonight was chill, but it was too early in the season to turn the heaters on yet—they took a day or two to really start kicking in and warming the house, so there was never any point just turning them on for an evening.

The aroma of wild mushrooms perfumed the air, meaty and savoury and somehow just a little more delicate and complex than store-bought portobellos—they'd spotted some of the milk caps on the side of the road after all, as they'd been leaving the forest, and after the kids had gone to sleep, Russell had fried them up with butter and tried them on toast, a willing canary testing the safety of their find. His verdict had been positive, and Lily had to admit that they'd smelled pretty amazing. Maybe they'd try again in another couple of days; the rain had settled in as they'd driven home, and that was supposed to be good for bringing a new crop of mushrooms up.

The TV droned on, some YouTube channel Russell was into at the moment about remaking old cars and such.

"Hmm?" Russell murmured idly, tilting his head toward Lily.

"The pouch thingy," she said, nodding toward the kitchen where her shiny, lime-green find still sat in the makeshift picnic bag. "I don't know. I've never seen anything like it, I'm not sure what it is, and I just feel like someone is going to be missing it."

"Sure, honey," Russell agreed. "Stick it up in the local BSS group or something."

Lily nodded firmly and reached out to snag her laptop off the nearby coffee table.

It was a matter of minutes to open her browser, find a local Buy-Swap-Sell group on Facebook that seemed promising, and post a message about the object she'd found.

She didn't add a photo; she deliberated over that decision, but in the end a photo was more likely to attract collectors who wanted to claim… whatever it was, simply because it was there, and it was unusual.

Smallish green pouch, reasonably heavy, found in pine plantation out past Urriara. PM for more details.

If the real owner was looking for it, they'd know what she meant.

It would have to do.

As Lily sat at her desk with her over-sized headphones on and a mint-scented candle burning nearby, the sharp 'ding' of a notification on her laptop sent her scrambling for the mute button, both on the laptop itself and on the zoom meeting she was currently 'participating' in.

Reading articles about local mushrooms while listening to the call was participating, right?

And anyway, her team leader was only telling them exactly the same information the boss had emailed two days prior, it was nothing new—confirmed: out of the office for the next four weeks, office phones diverted so they'd send voicemails as email, make sure you don't contact clients out of hours, ensure that you take time to exercise regularly and sign off on your work health and safety paperwork before next Tuesday, et cetera, et cetera, blah blah.

Honestly, Lily was so sick of zoom she'd stab herself in the eyeball if she thought it would do any good, but the bosses were treating it like it was the best Christmas gift they'd ever had, so here she was. But if she was going to be stuck on calls that did nothing more than repeat information she already had, darn it all if she wasn't going to make good, multitasking use of the time.

And so, mushroom research it was.

It was at least as productive as listening to Alfred whine about how his desk chair at home didn't lower to the correct height; the kids had gone to sleep like a dream last night after spending a few hours running around in the bush, so as soon as the rain let up again, they'd go back and roam around some more, look for some more mushrooms, that sort of thing.

Assuming she didn't get fired, of course, for her bloody computer ding-ing notifications at her on a business call.

Mind you, Sally's cat had plonked itself right on top of Sally's keyboard last week, right as she was supposed to be demonstrating a fiddly new proce-dure to the rest of the team, and she hadn't even been reprimanded, so perhaps a computer ding was just par for course these days.

Still, Lily scrolled through her open tabs as Alfred blathered on, trying to find the source of the interruption so she could avoid future embarrassment.

Ah, Facebook. That was why she didn't recognise it.

Trying to look like she was utterly intent on Alfred's chair issues, Lily opened her messages and found the source of the notification: someone had messaged her about the bizarre green pouch.

A Margaret A, who, judging by her profile picture, was maybe in her fifties and probably loved cats, and had two probable-grandchildren who looked to be about the same age as Lily's kids.

Hello, Lily. Is the green pouch you found shiny sort of chartreuse, soft leather, about 15cm long?

For no discernible reason, Lily's pulse sped up.

Yes.

Three dots popped up, bobbing up and down as Margaret A typed out a response.

And you found it in the Blue Rocks Waterhole Plantation, near the corner of East-West Rd and Blue Rocks Rd?

...That seemed plausible? Lily bit her lip, then, fighting the urge to bring up a map and double check, typed, *Yes.*

Is the pouch still sealed?

Lily felt like she was getting repetitive, but nevertheless, *Yes,* she typed—then added, *It is,* just for some variation. Was it still sealed? Heck if she knew how to open the thing.

Ah, lovely, Margaret replied, almost immediately. Fast typer, if nothing else. *What is your address, and when is it convenient for me to collect it?*

Lily nearly smiled, then remembered she was faking interest in the work call. *Working from home these days - aren't we all? - so any time is fine.*

She added her address—and realised Alfred had stopped complaining
about his chair and their team leader
Scott was wrapping up the meeting.

Quickly, Lily flicked back over to the
zoom window, nodding sagely as
though Scott's final comments were
the most important thing she'd heard
in her life, and managed to wave a con-
vincing goodbye in approximate syn-
chronisation with everyone else before
leaving the meeting.

Phew.

She sat back in her chair and stared
for a moment at the flickering flame of
the minty candle, inhaling one of her
favourite scents deeply and tilting her
head sharply to one side. Her neck
cracked satisfyingly.

Right.

Facebook. Margaret A.

Lily swiped back to her browser again and saw Margaret's latest message:
Is 5pm tonight convenient?

The wording made Lily smile a little. *Yeah,* she replied. *5pm is fine.*

By the time 5pm rolled around, the rain had well and truly set in. It put a bit of a damper on any prospect of walking the kids around the pond, but they'd survive being locked up for a day. Thank goodness they'd had a big run yesterday.

They were now busily ensconced in front of the TV, playing a virtual gardening game on the Xbox that kept them entertained and at least was mostly free of violence.

The shower shushed in the ensuite where Russell was transitioning from work to home, and Lily bustled around the kitchen, loading the dishwasher and cleaning off the bench in preparation for making dinner. She wrinkled her nose at the smell in the sink—Benjamin had tipped cereal in there and a bunch of it had caught in the plug that sieved out garbage before it could run down the drain. Gross.

She twisted out the plug, shook it a few times to stop it dripping so much, then carried it in her cupped hand to the bin.

Someone knocked at the door.

Lily stared at the goop in her hands for a second, gave her head a little shake, and tapped the gross cereal remains into the rubbish. "Coming!" she shouted. Quickly, she dropped the plug back into the sink and rinsed her hands.

Drying them on a dishtowel that had been lying over the fruit bowl, Lily sniffed. At least the kitchen smelled better now, the scent of lemon cleaner overpowering most everything else.

At the front door, a woman with reddish-brown hair and careful, neat makeup stood a few paces away, hands clasped in front of her. Her baby-blue blouse was neatly pressed, her slacks crisp—although damp spatters around the cuffs proved she had, at least, walked to the front door instead of levitating, as her other-wise perfect appearance suggested.

"Hi," Lily said brightly as she opened the screen. "You must be Margaret."

Ah, there *was* an umbrella, a slightly whimsical clear plastic one, neatly folded behind the potted azalea, which was just starting to bear tightly-furled white buds.

The woman nodded. "You must be Lily."

Lily smiled as the aroma of rain-soaked earth curled around her. "Or-dinarily I'd ask you in. But these days…"

Margaret smiled in response, warm-th crinkling her dark eyes. "Of course.

I'm happy to wait here." She lifted a hand a little, gesturing at the roof covering the entryway.

"Just a sec." Lily ducked back down the hall and in to the master bedroom. The bed was a mess, covers twisted and folded over themselves—Russell had reverted to his natural sleep patterns, i.e. 1am to 10am, and rarely remembered to straighten the bed out when he got up, not that Lily min-ded—and the lime-green pouch sat on Lily's bedside table, perched some-what precariously on a stack of crisp, new paperbacks.

Russell's cucumber-scented shower gel wafted out from the ensuite on the warm, damp air of the shower. Snat-ching up the pouch, Lily closed her eyes briefly to enjoy the warm air, then headed back to the front door.

"This is your pouch?" she said, holding it up to show Margaret as she opened the screen door again.

Goosebumps rose on her arms; the air out here was markedly cooler than in the bedroom.

Margaret's whole appearance was one of control and collectedness, but even so the relief in her eyes was palpable as she reached for the pouch. "Yes," she said. "That's it."

The way she took it, cradling it in both hands as though it was, perhaps, a small baby, caused Lily to tilt her head. "Do you mind if I ask how you lost it?"

Margaret made brief, nearly furtive, eye contact. "You didn't open it, did you." Statement, not question.

"No," Lily said with a small, wry smile.

Margaret sighed deeply, pressed the pouch to her chest, then picked at the seam across the top with long, natural-pink nails—and voila, the thick threads of the seam unravelled, reminding Lily of the bulk cloth bags of rice you could buy from the supermarket that came with a zipper but were initially stitched closed, presumably to prevent accidental rice spillages in said supermarkets.

The tucked-in ends of the pouch that had been sewn shut opened out, and then Margaret tipped up the pouch, spilling the contents into one cupped hand.

Small, bluish-grey rocks, rough and raw but with a gorgeous intensity to their colour.

Lily's eyebrows shot up.

"It was stupid of me," Margaret said, and abruptly Lily realised just how much of Margaret's mannerism and appearance were at odds with what she'd expected of someone who had lost a pouch in a remote pine forest where mushrooms were found. "But my grandchildren—my granddaughter, it was her birthday on Tuesday, and of course we couldn't have a party with the pandemic going on, so we decided to head out to the forest. She'd just been reading Small Mice, Big Mushrooms, you know that new children's book?"

Lily nodded; she did, in fact, know the book Margaret was referring to, because Benjamin had been watching readings of it obsessively on YouTube last week and that's half the reason Russell had got it into his head to take the family mushroom hunting in the first place.

She grinned. "I bet your granddaughter couldn't wait to go mushroom hunting after that."

Margaret's eyebrows rose mildly. "Your children too?"

Lily nodded and leaned against the doorframe, shifting her weight onto her left leg and crossing her right one over. "And my husband."

Margaret grinned at that one, an infectious expression that lit up her eyes and made her seem much younger. "This," she said, lifting the hand full of rocks, "was supposed to be my birthday present to her. I was going to hide them under a tree or two and let the kids go fossicking. But by the time we carried all the things down out of the car, the pouch had fallen out, and we couldn't find it anywhere." She shook her head. "I was so mad at myself. These," she added, wriggling the fingers that held the rocks, "were not cheap, you know."

"What it is?" Lily asked, staring again at the blue rocks.

"Ah."

Lily glanced up. Margaret hadn't actually *blushed* per se, but she certainly seemed... abashed.

"Well. You see, it's her tenth birthday, double digits and all, a bit special, and she's been very interested in rocks and stones and geology since she was six, so, uh... They're sapphires."

Lily's eyes widened. "What, all of them?" she blurted. There were what, six, seven… eight. Eight rocks about the size of the tip of her pinky sitting there in Margaret's hand, and sure, they'd shrink down a lot if they were cut and polished, but holy cow.

Holy *cow*.

"It's rather extravagant, I know," Margaret murmured, gaze downcast. "You must understand"—she met Lily's eye very briefly—"I never had much growing up. My parents lived through the Great Depression, they both worked two jobs each to make ends meet. I just…"

Lily softened, offered Margaret a warm, gentle smile. "You just wanted your grandkids to have a better life than you did," she said.

"Yes." Margaret's expression turned grateful.

"I understand," said Lily.

"Thank you." Margaret's hand curled around the stones, and carefully, she let them drop out of her fist and back into the pouch. "I very much appreciate it."

One stone lingered between forefinger and thumb, catching what little light there was from the overcast sky, looking like a piece of the rainclouds had come down and solidified here in Margaret's hand.

Margaret stretched out the stone toward Lily. "I want you to have this."

"What? I... No, I can't possibly. That's far too much."

"Take it," Margaret said, lifting the uncut sapphire higher. "I insist. As you can see, I have no shortage here."

Lily swallowed, eyes on the stone. "Margaret. Really?" She searched Margaret's face, left eye, right eye, the lips with their perfectly applied colour pressed slightly together. "You can't."

"I can, and I insist," Margaret said, nodding. "Please. You've saved me so much."

Lily stretched out her hand.

The stone landed in it, lightweight enough but holy cow, an entire uncut sapphire the size of her pinky tip.

Margaret grinned. "It's worth about twenty dollars," she said, wrapping the loose strings of the pouch tightly around its mouth.

Some strange sort of relief drenched Lily's body; she realised her pulse had sped up, adrenalin zinging around her system at the prospect of the stone.

Twenty dollars.

She sagged a little against the door post. That was a much, *much* more reasonable reward for her efforts. "Thank you," she said, injecting as much of that into her tone as she could.

Margaret's smile, soft and broad and bright-eyed, said she understood.

"You're more than welcome. Did your family find any mushrooms?"

Lily laughed. "Yes, we did, and my husband ate them and hasn't died yet, so I think we did okay."

Margaret nodded. "Well done. Your children are lucky to have parents like you."

A warm blush stole through Lily's chest. "And your grandkids are lucky to have you."

Margaret said goodbye, snapped open her umbrella against the rain, and Lily went back into the house, tucking the blue stone into the pocket of her jeans. Maybe she'd get it set into a pendant or something. It certainly wouldn't hurt to have a reminder of that one, perfect afternoon of silver-bright silence and space with her family in the midst of the chaos of the world.

THE MAKING OF *MORE THAN MUSHROOMS*

More Than Mushrooms, once called *Blue Rocks*, was another one of those stories I wrote in April 2020 during Canberra's first lockdown for my 10-stories-in-20-days challenge. (I wrote six in fourteen days, as you'll know if you've read the other relevant Inklets and/or the final collection of them, *April Showers*.)

I also wrote this for a course I was doing at the same time, and I was required to write a non-fantasy, non-science fiction mystery.

I'd never done that before, and afterward I still felt quite uncertain about whether or not I'd achieved the specific brief I'd been given… but I did quite like the story.

The moment in the forest is almost directly lifted from real life. During that first lockdown, the remote-ish state forests were somewhat of a reprieve for our family of four, somewhere we could go away from the crowds where the kids could run and we could breathe without fear of what we might inhale.

Alack, we did not find anything of financial value in the forests during those wanders. We did, though, gain plenty of non-financial value—and apparently, material for a short story.

Which just goes to show that value comes in many forms and really, it can be found anywhere.

Here's to finding plenty of blue rocks, financially valuable or otherwise, in your own life, as often as you can.

Read more by Amy Laurens!

CRYSTALLINE AND BRIGHT

I stood, staring down into the teal-blue river water, ignoring the chatter behind my back. The snow covered the ground around me, hiding bumps and ridges, soothing out sharp edges. To my right, the dark stone shadow of the bridge stood like a guardian, watchful, alert. Snow rimmed its edges; every so often some shifted in a sudden breeze and landed in the quiet river below with a gentle splash.

The willows on the far bank slept quietly under their snow blanket, their green sappy smell hidden by the cold, sharp scent of the snow.

Stop.

Start again.

It wasn't actually winter. It was early spring, with the grass green and new, the sound of a lawnmower buzzing in the distance and the scent of cut grass drifting on the wind. Moss covered the shadowed side of the old stone bridge, and willows stretched their fingers to the slow-moving, drowsy little river that bordered the grounds of the school.

A butterfly flittered past, white wings speckled with black like soot.

The world felt fresh, and green, and full of promise.

I was still ignoring the chattering behind me.

Stop.

Start again.

It's summer, and the air is swelteringly hot. Sweat drips down the back of my neck, pools under my arms, under my awkward breasts. The river in front of me is milky-blue, gentle, quiet, and I long to strip off my shirt and jeans and throw myself into the water.

It's not just the breathtakingly sharp cold of the icemelt I'm craving; it's the feeling of being *clean*.

The air stinks of a fish that Lander left out on the bank near the bridge, rotting to pieces in the high temperatures.

I'm still ignoring the chatter.

Stop.

Let's try once more.

It's autumn—of course—and the willows have turned yellow, their little leaves dropping into the milk-water, eddying slowly away from the shadow of the bridge.

Behind me, the emerald lawn of the old school buildings is ringed with gem-toned maples, butter-leafed poplars, silver-and-gold birches. Occasionally, the wind catches stray leaves and flings them into the pond.

I can still hear the voices behind me.

All of these pictures are true, and none of them are.

Not precisely, not uniquely; they're all composites, the merging and piecing together of hundreds of memories of similar experiences, of all the times I stood on the river bank and stared longingly into its depths, imagining myself a naiad with a secret home to return to, somewhere people loved me.

These images have to be composites, because for every time I was down at the river, I was focusing only on two things: ignoring the voices, and watching the water.

All the other details, the little bits of specificity that allow me to recall the place in so much explicit detail? I never noticed them at the time.

And so I have to piece them together, collage-fashion, or else I have nothing to say. Nothing to see.

Nothing except the water, milky-blue that occasionally, in the right light, at the right time of day, flashed teal and came alive.

I'd lived with the voices as long as I could remember. Some of them were real, inasmuch as they belonged to real, live people whom other people could see, who grew and developed and changed with the passing of the seasons; some of them were *surreal*, inasmuch as they belonged to people I could see, but that none other could, and who did not change or grow with the passing of the seasons.

And some of the voices... Some of them I could never divine exactly what they were.

But all of them, real, surreal and unknown, had one thing in common: none of them liked me.

I could never figure out why. Oh, sure, I came to the school without the name and pedigree of any of the other students, a supposed-orphan with no memory of her life before double digits and no connections to speak of. I wasn't part of their circle, my excellent trust fund notwithstanding, and so the real people, the live people, couldn't accept me.

It shouldn't have been that way. It seemed to me that I hadn't done anything wrong, or untoward, hadn't neglected to do anything needed, hadn't slighted or snubbed any who hadn't already done so several times to me.

And yet, for all the years I was there at the school, its grand, lofty double-storey buildings made from pale stone like a castle, ivy creeping all about like Christmas lights, the lawn constantly

emerald, the hedges consistently clip-
ped... For all those composite years,
no one ever liked me.

Well, a slight exaggeration: my tea-
chers liked me well enough. I was a
diligent student.

And the river liked me. I could tell
that, because when I was close to the
river, the other voices kept their distance—and the river had a voice of its
own. And once or twice, I could have
sworn it also had a face.

Keep reading! Head to
www.inkprintpress.com/
amylaurens/aprilshowers/
to buy your copy now!

ABOUT THE AUTHOR

AMY LAURENS is an Australian author of fantasy fiction for all ages. Her story *Bones Of The Sea*, about carnivorous Mist and cursed bones, won the 2021 Aurealis for Best Fantasy Novella.

Amy has also written the award-winning portal-fantasy *Sanctuary* series about Edge, a 13-year-old girl forced to move to a small country town because of witness protection (the first book is *Where Shadows Rise*), the humorous fantasy *Kaditeos* series, following newly graduated Evil Overlord Mercury as she attempts to acquire a castle, the young adult series *Storm Foxes*, about love and magic and family in small town Australia, and a whole host of short stories and non-fiction.

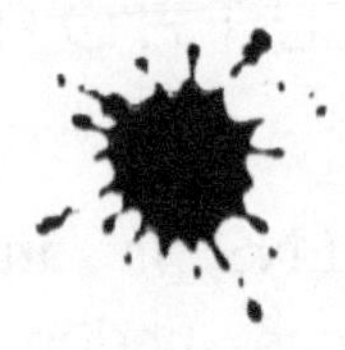

INKLETS

Collect them all! Released on the 1st and 15th of each month.

Dancer, Dreamer Seer
LIANA BROOKS

As Time Whirls Slowly Past
AMY LAURENS

Far More Satisfying Than Hell
AMY LAURENS

Just Another Day In Hell
LIANA BROOKS

Moon and Morning
AMY LAURENS

Some Impropriety Expected
AMY LAURENS

NEON SNOW
LIANA BROOKS

Reincarnation
LIANA BROOKS

More Than Mushrooms
AMY LAURENS

DOUBLE ISSUE
INKLET #092
How To Make A Star
& The World Ended
LIANA BROOKS

INKLET #093
CAUGHT
IN THE ACT
AMY LAURENS

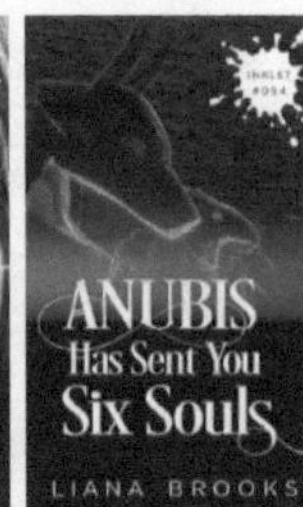

INKLET #094
ANUBIS
Has Sent You
Six Souls
LIANA BROOKS

INKLET #095
PRAYER TO A
GODDESS
LIANA BROOKS

INKLET #096
Love In The
Time Of Corona
AMY LAURENS

INKLET #097
RECRUITMENT
AMY LAURENS

INKLET #098
IDENTITY
Theft 101
LIANA BROOKS

INKLET #099
Curses
With Benefits
AMY LAURENS

INKLET #100
NECROMANCER
TROUBLES
LIANA BROOKS